This is Batpants the ora

She lives with Tilly and her brothers, Finn and Zak.

When they're together things can go a little bit ape!

Jeremy Strong once worked in a bakery, putting the jam into three thousand doughnuts every night. Now he puts the jam in stories instead, which he finds much more exciting. At the age of three, he fell out of a first-floor bedroom window and landed on his head. His mother says that this damaged him for the rest of his life and refuses to take any responsibility. He loves writing stories because he says it is 'the only time you alone have complete control and can make anything happen'. His ambition is to make you laugh (or at least snuffle). Jeremy Strong lives near Bath with his wife, Gillie, four cats and a flying cow.

Are you feeling silly enough to read more?

LAUGH YOUR Socks off with

Jeremy STRONG

Batpants!

Illustrated by Rowan Clifford

PUFFIN

Special thanks to stuntwoman extraordinaire Sarah Franzl,
whose help and advice was both entertaining and indispensable

PUFFIN BOOKS

Published by the Penguin Group
Penguin Books Ltd, 80 Strand, London WC2R 0RL, England
Penguin Group (USA) Inc., 375 Hudson Street, New York, New York 10014, USA
Penguin Group (Canada), 90 Eglinton Avenue East, Suite 700, Toronto, Ontario, Canada M4P 2Y3
(a division of Pearson Penguin Canada Inc.)
Penguin Ireland, 25 St Stephen's Green, Dublin 2, Ireland (a division of Penguin Books Ltd)
Penguin Group (Australia), 250 Camberwell Road, Camberwell, Victoria 3124, Australia
(a division of Pearson Australia Group Pty Ltd)
Penguin Books India Pvt Ltd, 11 Community Centre, Panchsheel Park, New Delhi – 110 017, India
Penguin Group (NZ), 67 Apollo Drive, Rosedale, North Shore 0632, New Zealand
(a division of Pearson New Zealand Ltd)
Penguin Books (South Africa) (Pty) Ltd, 24 Sturdee Avenue, Rosebank, Johannesburg 2196, South Africa

Penguin Books Ltd, Registered Offices: 80 Strand, London WC2R 0RL, England

puffinbooks.com

First published 2010
1

Text copyright © Jeremy Strong, 2010
Illustrations copyright © Rowan Clifford, 2010
All rights reserved

The moral right of the author and illustrator has been asserted

Set in Baskerville
Made and printed in England by Clays Ltd, St Ives plc

British Library Cataloguing in Publication Data
A CIP catalogue record for this book is available from the British Library

ISBN: 978-0-141-32796-9

www.greenpenguin.co.uk

Penguin Books is committed to a sustainable future
for our business, our readers and our planet.
The book in your hands is made from paper
certified by the Forest Stewardship Council.

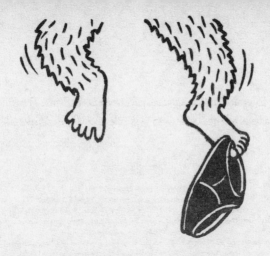

This is for Rosa and Izzy, who have never ever
had a book dedicated to them before.
They aren't the least like orang-utans either, even though
their mother has suspiciously longer-than-average arms.

Contents

1 Batpants and Other Family Members

I live in a tree house. You may wonder why.
Could it be:

1   because my parents don't have a proper house?

2   because my parents didn't like to have us kids in their house because we're too noisy and messy?

3   because a gigantic strawberry cheesecake had fallen out of the sky, landed on our house and smashed it to bits and we had to live *somewhere*?

4   because Dad was very clever and thought that Finn and Zak

and I would really, really, really
LIKE to live in a tree house, so he
built one for us?

Guess what the answer is? Of course. It's 4.

The tree house is connected to the main home
by a wooden walkway that wiggles across to the
upstairs hallway. We have a dangly rope hanging
down to the ground. (There are wooden stairs
too, but the rope is a lot more fun.)

Finn is seven and a small pain. Zak is thirteen,
and a big pain. Then there's me, Tilly – I'm ten.
(And definitely no pain at all.) Oh, and I mustn't
forget our orang-utan.

Dad trains animals for films and TV. You
remember the advert where a tiger sits in a car
and seems to drive it? Well, the tiger was trained
to do that by our dad, and it was Dad who
brought our orang-utan over from Borneo. He'd
been filming there. She was just a baby then, and

an orphan too.

Dad looked after her. He couldn't bear to leave her behind when filming finished so he got permission and brought her home to us. We fell in love with her at once. She was so *cute*! Even when she tiddled on your lap. It wasn't her fault — even human babies do that.

Mind you, it did help when Mum got some disposable nappies for her. She looked so funny, waddling about the house like some incredibly hairy little old man who'd been put in a washing machine and come out all shrunken. And with very long arms. And wearing a nappy.

Do you know what the most difficult thing about having an orang-utan in the house is? I'll tell you – trying to think up a good name for her.

'Gingernut,' said Zak.

'Mabel,' I offered.

'Hairybum,' Finn suggested, and went into squeals of laughter. (He was only five at the time.)

'Floretta,' said Mum, which mystified us. She held up her hands and explained. 'I had a great-aunt called Floretta and she was rather similar to an orang-utan.'

'But Floretta makes her sound like a bit of broccoli,' I complained.

'Anyway, how did your great-aunt look like an orang-utan?' asked Zak.

'She was rather hairy,' Mum told us, stroking her chin, which sent Finn into more squeals.

Then Dad came up with his suggestion.

'Lady Henrietta Withering Gas-Trumpett,' he

announced. We looked at him in despair. And we still couldn't think of a good name.

One day Finn was playing at being Batman. He didn't have a proper costume, but I gave him a pair of my old tights.

Finn pulled on his grey school jumper and a pair of wellingtons for his bat-boots. His cloak was a black bin liner. Batman's pants were a problem, though. Finn didn't have any black pants, so we found a pair of Dad's Y-fronts.

Gross. Don't worry, they were clean, but totally uncool.

'Just don't poo in them,' I warned.

'I'm not TWO and Batman does not poo his pants!' shouted Finn.

The orang-utan came in to see what all the noise was about and my brain just about burst with the best idea ever.

'Why don't we dress *her* as Batman!'

Quick as a flash the tights came off Finn and went on the ape. So did the school jumper. We decided the boots wouldn't work. Instead, we draped her in Batman's cloak. That just left the pants.

I don't think orang-utans like wearing pants. Ours snatched the Y-fronts from me and stuck them on her head, pulling the sides right down over her face. Her nose and one eye peeped out from a leg hole. An ear poked through the other.

The ape stood there, gazing at us with the one bewildered eye. This was the superhero who was supposed to SAVE THE WORLD! With pants on her head!

It was just too funny. Finn and I fell about. That was when the ape set off at high speed, zooming round the house. She whizzed upstairs, downstairs and through all the rooms, hooting like crazy. 'Hoo hoo whaaaa!'

She only came to a halt when she went hurtling straight into Zak, almost knocking him over.

Zak looked down at the sprawling animal, busily wrestling a pair of Y-fronts on her head. 'WHO or WHAT is THAT?' he asked.

'Batman,' I said. 'Obviously.'

'Bat-*MAN*?' snorted Zak. 'If you ask me, she looks more like Bat-*PANTS*!'

Finn and I looked at each other.

It was the perfect name.

2 Escaped Bushes and Major Hair Accidents

Batpants has small ears, big eyes and an even bigger mouth, which she loves to fill. She likes apple crumble, roast chicken and small tomatoes.

She eats the apple crumble and chicken, but she doesn't eat the tomatoes. Instead she likes to load them into her mouth. Then she purses her lips and blows the tomatoes back out at high speed, like a machine gun.

RATTA – SPLATTA – SPLATTA!

Mum and Dad have banned Batpants from shooting people with tomatoes, but Finn and I still smuggle her some when we can. We usually eat in the big kitchen so you can probably guess that the walls are a bit messy now. There's a very interesting tomato-pippy effect splattered across them. Visitors often spend hours staring at the walls, trying to work out how it was done. We don't tell them.

Batpants managed to hit Zak once, right in

the middle of his forehead. *SPLAPP!* Finn and I
thought that was the most brilliant thing EVER.

You may think that it's odd to have a pet
orang-utan who
machine-guns
people with
tomatoes, but in
fact they are very
brainy beasts.
They're clever
with their hands
and feet too.
They could pick
their noses with
their toes if they
felt like it. Luckily,
they don't often
feel like it.

Besides, for us, Batpants was just another of
the animals we have around the place. We have
three cats – Cookie, Crumpet and Teacake.

Then there's Horse the donkey (Zak's joke),
and Twiglet the giant stick insect (Dad's joke).
We also have a bearded dragon lizard known as

 Betty, and some
frogspawn called
– guess what –
frogspawn.

As if that's not
enough, there
is also Finn's
private collection
of interesting
creatures. He
collects things
like earwigs,
beetles, worms,
woodlice, spiders,

caterpillars and anything that's small enough and
slow enough for him to capture. (Yes, I know, he's
VERY strange, but he's my little bro so I just have
to put up with it.) He mostly keeps them in boxes,

but he's not much good at remembering where he's put them. The earwigs might turn up on top of the television. The worms could be enjoying the bathtub.

This gets Finn into trouble, especially with Zak, who doesn't like discovering unexpected caterpillars in his coat pocket. It doesn't suit his rock-star image. If you ever meet Zak he will

soon tell you that he is going to be HUGE on the music scene. His guitar playing is certainly loud enough. Dad says it makes his teeth rattle. Zak's got his own band – *The Non-Organic Vegetables.*

'Why "non-organic"?' asked Mum.

'It's more threatening,' Zak answered threateningly.

Zak has long, straight purple and black hair that he keeps having to flick back otherwise he can't see. He walked into his bedroom door once. *BANG! OW!* Almost everything he wears is black and his T-shirt says 'DEATH' in big letters on the front. Because of Zak's loud guitar playing Dad reckons it's a spelling mistake and it's supposed to say 'DEAF'.

Then there's Zak's famous black coat. It comes right down to his boots and flows behind him like a dark cloud. Finally, he has a silver stud through his left eyebrow. (Ouch!) It kind of upset Mum and Dad.

'Oh, Zak,' moaned Mum. 'What did you do that for?'

'It's cool,' Zak said.

'It's ugly,' Dad corrected.

'Ugly is the new cool,' answered Zak.

I'm not like either of my brothers, thank goodness. I'm ten and I'm really into eco-stuff like saving whales. I'd like to adopt one and have it at home, but the pond's not big enough. I like to feel that I'm at one with Nature, you know? So I paint my face in earth and leaf colours. I don't like itty-pretty necklaces and stuff so

I decorate myself with plants and feathers instead.

Zak once told me I looked like an escaped bush.

'So?' I snapped back. 'You look like a Major Hair Accident, but don't worry – I'll call an ambulance and they can take you to the Emergency Hair Hospital.' Ha ha! That shut him up.

Anyhow, that's way too much about us. I want to tell you about our life with exploding buildings and karate penguins, not to mention when Mum almost got squeezed to a squodge.

3 Fantasti-bubbly-crumbo!

Emma Lovehart – that's my mum – used to be a brilliant gymnast. She's got a whole shelf full of trophies she's won in competitions. She's also a great swimmer and can swim forty metres underwater. That means WITHOUT BREATHING! Plus, she knows how to make the best chocolate cake EVER. Yummy crumby!

Mum's small and pretty, with big kind hazel eyes. No wonder Dad married her! Dad's from Turkey and he's called Aslan. That means *lion* in Turkish. Obviously, he's not a real lion, but he does look like one. He's got a big mane of swept-back hair. He also has a largish nose and silver-rimmed spectacles. Lions have large noses too, but they don't wear spectacles and if they did they would have to be wrap-around, mirror-lens sunglasses or they'd just look stupid.

When I started junior school a few kids teased me because my dad was Turkish. It's the sort of dumb thing kids say when they don't know any better. I said everyone had to come from somewhere. Obviously.

'Yes, but *yours* comes from *Turkey*,' Evie sniped. She's bossy like that.

'So where does your dad come from?' I asked, and when Evie said 'Pratts Bottom' the whole class fell about laughing. We didn't even believe it until my friend Sandeep found it on a map. Evie didn't tease me after that.

Anyhow, back to Mum. She's a stuntwoman in films and television. Stuntwomen (and men) do all sorts of dangerous things like jumping out of aeroplanes and falling down stairs. So Mum isn't a mega-zonic big-screen star like Victoria Sponge or Tiara Tingletop, but when they have to do something dangerous Mum does the dangerous bit for them. Three cheers for my mum!

Suppose Victoria Sponge is making a movie where she goes hurtling over a thunderous waterfall in a tiny canoe. Victoria doesn't do that herself – it's far too dangerous. A stunt actor does it instead. Stunt actors do special training so they can carry out these things without getting hurt.

Mum dresses up to look like Victoria and *she* goes hurtling over the waterfall instead. She's always doing extraordinary things like that. She had to fight six penguins once, and they weren't ordinary penguins. Dad had trained them all to do karate. Picture the scene – black belt

karate penguins! How scary is that? This scary –

AAAAAAAAAAAAAAARRRGGGGH!

So one morning at breakfast Mum came into the kitchen and said, 'I'm working on a new film.'

We stopped eating, food halfway to our mouths, not knowing what to expect. Did that mean she was going to be away from home for weeks again? (Groan groan.)

'It's OK. I don't have to stay in America this time. I'll be filming over here and –' She paused for effect, knowing we were hanging on her every word.

'What?' shouted Finn.

'What?' I repeated impatiently.

Zak tossed back his hair. 'Spit it out, Mum,' he muttered.

'Well, since you're on holiday from school I thought you could come with me.' She smiled and handed Batpants a slice of toast. Toast and jam is another favourite.

'Result!' Zak relaxed back into his seat.

'Unbelievable,' I said.

Zak gave me an evil glance. 'The only unbelievable thing in this kitchen, Tilly, is your head. Why do you have half a bird's nest in your hair?'

'Obviously, so the birds will know I don't mean them any harm,' I declared.

Zak looked at the others. 'She's out of her

tree,' he muttered. 'And so is that nest.'

'*Taisez-vous*,' I snapped back. That's French, that is. Very cool. This is how you say it – *tayzay voo*. Guess what it means? *Shut up!* Very useful. We had a French student staying with us last year. Zak fell in love with her, of course. He's always falling in love. I think there's something wrong with him, like his brain, or his eyes, or both.

Anyhow, Zak would look at her and murmur, '*Marie*,' because that was her name, obviously. Marie kept telling him to '*Taisez-vous!*' Now I use it on Zak and Finn all the time.

'WHAT ABOUT THE FILM?' yelled Finn, almost bouncing off his chair. 'Can we be in it?'

Mum shrugged. 'You know what it's like, Finn. That would be great, but it's not up to me. There's the film director, Alana, who would have to decide. Still, you'll get to be on location at Murkley Abbey.'

She put some more jam on a knife and handed it to Batpants. The ape carefully spread the jam on to her toast, then shoved the whole lot in her mouth in one go.

'Is it another Colorado Kate movie?' asked Finn.

'Of course. *Colorado Kate and the Curse of the Crimson Chameleon*. Just for once the crew will be filming over here.'

The Colorado Kate films are about a daredevil adventuress, starring Frangelika Wotnot as Kate. Kate is always getting captured, or chased, or she's fighting bears, monsters, zombies, vampires, whatever.

When Colorado Kate runs away, she always loses a shoe or twists her ankle. *Oh no! Now she can't run fast enough! Colorado stumbles! Colorado falls! The bear-monster-zombie-vampire-whatever will surely catch her and then Colorado will DIE!*

As if! Kate always saves herself in the nick of time because she is STRONG and CLEVER and GOOD. (And unbelievable.) Besides, she's usually rescued by her latest hunky boyfriend and collapses into his arms. *Smooch smooch, snog snog,* yuck yuck.

Anyhow, Frangelika Wotnot can't possibly do all that awfully dangerous and messy stuff. She only does the safe bits like the snogging (if you call that safe) because she is the STAR and she must NEVER get her hair in a MESS. So guess who DOES do all the dangerous stuff? That's right. Emma Lovehart, top stuntwoman and our mum. Ta-ra, ta-ra!

Mum often spends months filming and do you know what she does when she gets home? She sleeps under the kitchen table! Just for the first few days, anyway.

'I've spent the last three months doing stunts. I've been thrown off buildings, blown up, jumped from cars and have fought giant snakes. The only place I want to be now is somewhere I can't fall out of bed and nothing can land on top of me or try to kill me, plus some peace and quiet.' And she crawls under the table with armfuls of cushions and blankets, curls up and sleeps like a baby.

Now Mum was going to work on a new Colorado film and that meant she would be standing in for Frangelika Wotnot. I mean, FRANGELIKA WOTNOT! She is about as peachy as anyone can get.

'We might get to meet her,' I whispered to Finn, but he wasn't listening. Something was bothering him.

'What about Batpants? Who's going to look after her?' he asked.

'Plooop-plooop-plooop,' complained the orang-utan. Sometimes I think she understands every word we say.

Dad chucked several more pieces of toast into the bread basket. They were instantly snaffled, mostly by Zak. 'It's not a problem. Batpants is in the film too.'

I was outraged. 'How come a useless orangutan gets to be in the film and we don't? That's not fair!'

Dad shrugged. 'Life is never fair, Tilly,' he said.

'You always say that,' grumbled Zak.

'Because it's true, and we deal with it. I thought you'd be pleased about Batpants.'

'I'm pleased!' cried Finn, pushing his hands against the table edge and leaning back on his chair. 'I think it's absolutely fantasti-bubbly-crumbo! Aaargh!'

The chair legs slid away from him and crashed to the floor. Finn clawed wildly at the table to save himself before vanishing completely from sight, pulling the cloth with him. Two cereal bowls, the milk, the bread basket, jam pot, sugar bowl and three side plates vanished with him.

KRRACKKK!
KERRUNCH!! SPINNGG!
SKRROWWKK!

For a few moments there was silence, then
Batpants covered her eyes with both arms.
'Whoooooooo!' she moaned.

A hand reached up from below and clutched the table again. A cereal bowl appeared, upside down, on top of Finn's head. Finally his face came into view, dripping with milk. Bits of cereal were stuck in his hair.

'Sorry?' he pleaded.

Mum lifted the bowl from his head and put it to one side. 'You can tidy up,' she sentenced, like a judge. 'Rubbish and breakages into the bin. Sweep and mop the floor. Do the washing-up *and* drying-up. Batpants behaves better than you.'

The ape heard her name and lowered her arms from her face. She picked up the jam knife and used it to inspect her left armpit as if it was something very important and serious that she had to attend to.

'On second thoughts that orang-utan is just as bad,' muttered Mum, changing her mind. 'She can help too.'

4 The Greatest Stuntwoman in the World?

Let me tell you that a film set is a strange place. First of all it's mostly pretend. The buildings often only have a front because that's all you see in the film. You walk through a front door and immediately you're outside again. There's stuff lying about everywhere – cars, cranes, pianos, plastic hippos, fountains, giant cakes, half a ship – it could be anything.

And there are real film stars wandering about, right in front of you! You know, the people you read about in magazines.

Victoria Sponge poses on the red carpet at last night's Oscar ceremony.

Handsome hunk, Manley Strutt, relaxing in his Jacuzzi.

Finn and I love it. We wander about, trying to sneak into film sessions by mingling with the extras in crowd scenes. Sometimes we're spotted and get

thrown out (rats!), but occasionally we've ended up in the actual movie. I've been in two films already. But we were especially excited to be on this film set, even Zak, who was trying to act cool.

As soon as we got to Murkley Abbey we went out for an explore. That meant all four of us – Batpants, Zak, Finn and me. We wandered about the place to see if any filming had started or maybe spot a few peachy film stars. It was pretty quiet, though.

Batpants was trailing behind us, swinging a big stick she had picked up. She kept banging it against the back of Zak's legs, trying to trip him

up. That got Zak SO angry and Finn and I fell about laughing.

'Will you stop that, you boneless bonehead!' Zak yanked the stick from Batpants and hurled it as hard as he could to one side. A second later there was a loud *CRUMPP!* as it hit the roof of a nearby caravan.

'Uh-oh,' murmured Finn, and Batpants covered her head and gave a low moan.

A door flew open and a woman came charging out. 'Was that you children? What did you throw at my home? Why have you got a baboon with you?'

'Sorry. It's Batpants,' said Zak, quickly inventing an excuse. 'She likes us to throw sticks for her.'

'And she's not a baboon,' I pointed out. I hate it when adults get things wrong. They're supposed to know better. 'She's an orang-utan.'

'I don't care if she's a meringue-utan,' barked the woman. 'Who are you, anyhow? I didn't think children were allowed here.'

Finn puffed out his chest. 'Our mum does Frangelika Wotnot's stunt work,' he declared proudly. 'She's the best stuntwoman in the world! She can fall down stairs and everything.'

The woman's eyebrows shot up her forehead like a couple of crows taking off. 'Is that so? Well, I can tell you that there's more than one stuntwoman on this set and I'm every bit as good as she is and I can prove it. Wait there.'

The woman whirled into her caravan, only to come hurtling back out a second later, clutching a picture frame. She thrust it at Zak. 'See what that says?'

We studied the photo, a signed portrait of film star Ethan Blade.

To Cressida Crappletart, a great stuntwoman,
from your friend Ethan Blade.

'See?' snapped Cressida. 'If I'm good enough for Ethan, I'm good enough for anyone. In fact, if anyone should be Frangelika's stuntwoman, it's me. You don't just fall down stairs, you know; you have to act.' She nodded. 'Yeah. And I've got a certificate for my acting.'

Huh! That didn't impress us. Anyone can have a certificate, and Finn told her so.

'I've got a certificate for swimming,' he said, 'but Zak's a better swimmer than me and he hasn't got a certificate for ANYTHING.'

'Not even playing the guitar,' I added. Smirk smirk.

'Bats can swim,' Finn put in for good measure,

'but hippos can't. They just sort of bounce.' We
ignored him. 'Underwater,' he added, in case we
hadn't understood. (I told you he was weird.)

Cressida Crappletart's eyes narrowed to dagger
points. 'What a pair of clever clogs,' she sneered.
She glared at us for a few seconds longer, then
went to take the photo back. Batpants had other
ideas. She whipped the photo away from Zak's
hand, planted a massive, slobbery kiss on Ethan
Blade's face and lurched off, whooping and
chattering.

'Hoo hoo HAARRR!' It was like she was
saying: 'Come and get me!'

Cressida Crappletart set off after the ape,
doing her own whooping. This was exactly what
Batpants wanted. She shot up a tree, hauling
herself up with easy swoops of her long arms.

'You come back down here, you overgrown
ginger mop!' shouted Cressida.

Batpants took no notice. She studied Ethan's
photo instead, tracing over his face with a long

brown finger. Cressida climbed into the tree and quickly worked her way up.

Batpants watched Cressida's approach. She scratched behind her left ear. She scratched behind her right ear. She bared her teeth.

'Don't pull faces at me, you scrawny hairbag!' Cressida warned.

Batpants turned her back on the stuntwoman, raised her bottom from the branch and made a very rude noise.

SPPPLURRGH!

'You disgusting dirtpot!' yelled Cressida. 'Just you come here and say that. On second thoughts, don't.'

At that point Batpants got bored and let go of the photo. It crashed down through several branches before lodging in a fork of the tree. Cressida grabbed it and climbed down.

'I'll be speaking to your mother about this,' she muttered, trying to clean ape-slobber from Ethan Blade's face.

'It's not our fault,' I said. 'You try telling an orang-utan what to do.'

'That's no excuse. She's a menace. She shouldn't be on the set.'

'She's in the film,' Zak stated bluntly. 'That's why she's here.'

Cressida Crappletart's mouth snapped shut. For a moment she was speechless. She spun on her feet and stormed back into her caravan, slamming the door behind her so hard the TV aerial fell off the roof.

I felt a fat, warm, hairy hand slide into mine. Batpants had slipped silently down from the tree and was back with us. She looked up at me with her huge, dark eyes as if to say: 'What's up with her? I am totally innocent.'

As we turned to go and find Mum I thought I saw the curtains at one of the windows on Cressida's caravan twitch. I wondered if she'd been watching us. That woman was KOOKY-SPOOKY.

Finn and I were trailing behind our big brother when he suddenly stopped dead. Finn walked straight into his rear. *SPLAMPFF!* Zak hardly noticed. He was staring, goggle-eyed, at someone coming straight towards us.

5 Strange Behaviour from a Pair of Mammals

A teenage girl. I should have known. A girl.

(I guess she did look OK, in a dopey kind of way.)

Zak's eyes were on stalks. Typical.

'She's pretty,' Finn whispered to me.

'Huh! You should get your eyes checked,' I muttered. 'She's got a face like a squashed spider. With mushy peas on top.'

Finn was dismayed. 'Why would you squash a spider with mushy peas? That's really cruel.'

I didn't have time to explain because Zak and the girl were making a beeline for each other and I wanted to see what happened. '*Taisez-vous!* Squashed-Spider Face is coming over.'

'Hi!' smiled the girl, showing perfect white teeth. 'Haven't seen you guys before.' She had

an American accent.

Zak goggled at her even more. You'd think he'd been hypnotized by her big green eyes. Maybe he was. She had long black hair and wore skinny jeans with a vest top.

Zak croaked a reply. 'Huh.'

I know, not really a reply at all, was it? They stood there gazing at each other. It reminded me of animal programmes on television. I sniggered and put on a low, serious voice to whisper to Finn.

'*The two humans meet in a clearing and communicate with each other by grunting. The female moves closer to inspect the male.*'

At that point, Squashed-Spider Face caught sight of Batpants, turned pale and started to back off.

'Is that baboon OK? I mean, is he safe?'

Safe? Baboon? Was the girl blind?

'SHE is an ORANG-UTAN,' I said sharply, while Batpants climbed up me and tried to play with the nest on my head. 'She's with us. She's kind of a pet.'

'Her name's Batpants,' Finn said proudly.

'That is so cool – a pet orang-utan.' The girl peered closely at my head. 'Did Batpants stick those twigs in your hair?'

'No, she didn't and they're not stuck, I put

them there,' I growled. 'On purpose.'

'She's a Flower Fairy,' chuckled Zak.

'NO, I AM NOT!' I folded my arms crossly. Zak can be such a pain. 'Actually, if you must know, I am an eco-warrior. I've got willow and feathers in my hair to show that I am in tune with Planet Earth. All right?'

'That's cool!' Squashed-Spider Face gave me a bright smile and, OK, she did look almost human when she smiled. She turned her gaze back to Zak. 'Nice coat.'

'Thanks,' said Zak. 'Nice –' he began, but couldn't think how to finish. He's hopeless with girls. No, I shall correct that. He's just hopeless, full stop. 'Nice – everything. Are you from round here?'

'Uh-huh.'

Zak pressed ahead. 'Me too.' They nodded at each other for a moment and then Zak added, ever so casually, 'I'm in a band.'

I started my TV documentary voice again. '*The*

male tries to get attention from the female by showing off while running his fingers through his purple mane.'

'In a band? Really?' smiled the girl. 'That's cool.'

Zak tossed his hair once more. 'Yeah – we're recording, you know? Like, you know, me and the band – recording?'

I went and stood beside him. 'He's in a band,' I repeated, in case Zak saying it twice wasn't enough. 'They're recording.'

The girl flashed her white teeth in another broad smile. 'I think I got that,' she giggled.

But Zak was not amused.

'Take no notice of her,' he swiped. 'She's just a baby.'

'Take no notice of him,' I parroted. 'He's waiting for a brain transplant.'

The girl laughed and shook her head. 'You guys! You're funny. So are you the guitarist? What do you play?'

'Thrash shed. The band's called The Non-

Organic Vegetables.'

'Cool,' said the girl admiringly. 'That's some name.'

They smiled at each other again and Zak blushed. I went back to whispering my animal commentary into Finn's ear. '*The male changes colour while the female plays with her hair.*'

Finn laughed and I tried to explain the name of Zak's band to the girl, sarcastically, of course. 'Organic vegetables are so wimpy, don't you think?'

Zak eyed me with annoyance. 'My little sister, Tilly the Silly. I'm Zak.'

'Zak the Yak,' I added, by way of getting even. 'And that's Finn.'

The girl stretched out a hand towards Zak. 'I'm Lacewing. Pleased to meet you guys.'

Finn suddenly looked more interested. 'Lacewings are insects,' he declared. 'You don't look like an insect.' (Actually, she did a bit. I mean, she was pretty long and thin. Bit like a millipede, but with only two legs.)

'Really?' Lacewing herself was surprised to hear this.

Finn nodded. 'Do you eat aphids? Because that's what lacewings eat.'

She looked to us for help. 'Aphids?'

'He's mad about creepy-crawlies,' I explained.

'I think it's a beautiful name,' said Zak, his voice too loud. His face went red again.

'I thank you, sir!' Lacewing gave a little curtsey. 'Did I tell you I sing?'

'Really?' Zak's face flushed more. 'I write music. Maybe you could sing with the Vegetables.'

'Yeah,' I murmured. 'You could be a singing potato.'

The girl laughed. 'Your little sister is a real comedian!'

'I AM NOT LITTLE!' I roared, and I was pleased to see her take three steps back.

Batpants chose that moment to amble forward,

wrap one long arm round Lacewing's leg and
park her backside on the girl's foot. Lacewing
pulled a face.

'Are you sure she's OK?'

'She likes you,' shrugged Finn.

'So does Zak,' I added. 'He'd like to sit on your
foot as well, but he's too shy.'

Zak snarled at me, so I stuck my tongue out at
him.

Lacewing laughed. 'So, is it like I'm auditioning for you then?'

'I guess,' nodded Zak.

'There's an empty caravan near me. We could maybe use that,' suggested Lacewing. 'Mom and I were in it for a bit, but it was so weeny, you wouldn't believe. Mom got us moved to a much bigger place.'

DURRR! I'd just put two and two together

and made a million. Surely this girl wasn't . . . No, she couldn't be . . . Surely not? I had to find out. 'Is your mother involved with Colorado Kate?' I tried to make it sound like a casual enquiry.

'You bet she is,' answered Lacewing. 'She's the main man – well, woman, of course.' She gave a little giggle.

My stomach turned inside out with excitement and I whispered to Finn. 'She must be Frangelika Wotnot's daughter! And she's going to sing in Zak's band! That is mega-zonic! And then they can get married and we'll all go to Hollywood! Result!'

Zak and Lacewing were so busy staring at each other with dopey eyes, they didn't hear any of this. Eventually, Lacewing asked Zak when they should meet up.

'Tomorrow morning,' Zak said. 'It'd be good to start right away, but our mum's filming this afternoon and we're going to watch. She's a stuntwoman. So we'll see you tomorrow?' he added hopefully.

'Sure thing,' smiled Lacewing. 'And, Zak, can I hear you play guitar sometime?'

'It'd just be me,' said Zak. 'The rest of The Vegetables aren't around.'

'Oh, I don't want to hear *them*,' Lacewing said coyly. 'Only you.'

Zak grinned as if he'd just won a shop full of chocolate. I clutched my stomach dramatically. 'Urrrgh – I feel ill,'

I groaned, and staggered up the path.

'Very funny, I don't think,' growled Zak, before brightening. 'Tomorrow's going to be brilliant. I can sense it. Totally brilliant.'

6 Rats!

Mum was filming in Murkley Abbey itself, which was an ancient, crumbling ruin of a place. It was hundreds of years old and looked about as cheerful as you would if you were that ancient. It was way too spooky – the sort of place where you expect to hear huge thunder bangs and crashing organ music being played by a mad goblin. So, probably not a good place to go for a holiday.

However, it was the perfect place for Colorado Kate to get chased by wolves, fall down ancient wells, discover dust-encrusted skeletons, have lots of desperate adventures, narrow escapes and generally almost DIE. (Just like she did in the last film, and the one before that, and the one before that, etc., etc.)

Mum and the film crew were down in a kind of cellar. Alana, the film's director, was talking to guess who? Frangelika Wotnot! I mean, actually talking to her, like she was a real person. Of course I know film stars are real people, but, you know, this was Frangelika Wotnot! I wouldn't have even dared to breathe near her, let alone speak to her.

'This is the abbey's crypt,' Alana was saying. 'It's where they kept dead bodies.'

'Is that right?' asked Frangelika, glancing at the rows of cobwebbed coffins. 'You mean there are still bodies in there?'

'Uh-huh,' nodded the director. 'Skeletons.'

Frangelika went very quiet.

'You only have to run between them,' Alana said encouragingly.

Frangelika took another look at the drooping curtains of cobwebs hanging from the coffins. She screwed up her nose. 'Can't Emma cover

that for me? She's supposed to do all that kind of stuff.'

I glanced at Mum and she winked back. Alana put a comforting hand on the film star's shoulder. 'It's not dangerous. All you do is run through it. We need to see your face.'

'It's all icky,' Frangelika complained. Honestly! Listening to her wittering on about a few cobwebs you'd think she was about three years old. Finn didn't help, either.

'Wow! Those webs are HUMONGOUS!' he suddenly piped up. 'The spiders in there must be mega-mugga-MASSIVE!'

A tiny whimper escaped from Frangelika. I shoved a hand over my smile. The film star had turned so deathly pale it looked like she ought to be climbing into one of the coffins herself.

'There are no spiders in there,' the director assured Frangelika.

'No?' she squeaked. 'But I'll get cobwebs all over me.'

'That's the whole point,' declared Alana. 'You are supposed to come out looking awful and terrified. Everyone in the cinema will look at you and *feel* for you, Frangelika. They will feel your fear and think, *Poor, poor Colorado Kate.*'

'They will?' Frangelika had another look at the sagging cobwebs. 'Can I have a shower *immediately* after?'

Alana sighed. 'When we've shot the scene, yes. Can we get on now? Let's have the orang-utan – oh! There you are!'

Batpants had already lurched across to join them. It was almost as if she knew she was needed. She reached out with a long arm and took hold of Frangelika's hand. The star smiled.

'You're such a cutie, aren't you, Batpants? Who's a boo-boo-booful babe? Now, don't you be a scaredy because Mamma is going to take you right through those icky sticky cobwebs, OK?'

I groaned. How could she talk to Batpants like that? She was hardly a baby.

'Quiet, everyone!' shouted Alana as Frangelika and Batpants moved into position.

I spotted Cressida Crappletart right

at the back of the crypt, lurking behind some
of the film crew. She was watching everything
intently. A shiver ran up my spine. I don't know
what it was about that woman, but she gave me
the heebie-jeebies.

'Cameras ready,' called the director. 'Frangelika,
all set to run through?'

'I guess,' whimpered the actress.

Alana sat back in her director's chair.
'Ready; action!'

Frangelika and Batpants plunged
towards the cobwebs. As she hit
them, Frangelika closed her eyes,
flailed her arms and screamed.

'Aaaaaaaaaaaaargh! I hate

this stuff!' She came bursting out at the other end, panting heavily and clawing wildly at the cobwebs that clung to every inch of her face and body.

'Purgh, purgh, purgh!' she spat. 'Where's that shower? Quick!'

'It's a wrap,' smiled the director. 'Showers are back at your caravan.'

'What?' screeched Frangelika. 'But my caravan's a mile away and . . . and look at me!' She stood there, arms straight by her sides as if she was waiting for someone to go over and start picking cobwebs off her.

Batpants was wandering round in circles, trailing cobwebs and making small *neep-neep* noises. She sounded like a distressed duck.

Mum went across to them both. 'Don't worry, Frange. You don't look too bad.' She helped brush the star down and gave her a tissue to wipe her face.

Meanwhile, Batpants clambered into Mum's

arms and clung to her like a small child. Frangelika smiled gratefully at Mum.

'Thanks, Em. You're a real friend – not like some around here.' Frangelika threw a cross glance at the director, who luckily wasn't even looking her way. 'Hey, Em, don't you do something awful now?'

Mum nodded. 'Big scene. I have to cross the rat-infested sewer.'

'Rather you than me. I don't know how you can stand those critters,' Frangelika said.

Mum laughed. 'Just between you and me, I can't.' That's typical Mum. She does all these crazy things and makes light of them. She is SO brave and when I actually saw the sewer I had to swallow really hard. It was like, you know, THE CHASM OF DEATH.

The sides were as steep as Mount Everest. Dark, slimy water oozed its way through the bottom. And there were dozens of rats, hundreds probably, swarming down there. The only way to cross the sewer was by a single, narrow beam of wood.

I thought Finn might like the rats since he seemed to be in love with horrible beasties. However, he took one look at them and rushed over to Mum. 'I don't want you to jump that,' he said. 'Don't do it, Mum, please.'

Mum hugged him. 'Finn, I do this sort of thing every day. All I do is run across that beam of wood there, you see it? Easy-peasy.'

Yeah, well, Mum would say it was easy-peasy, wouldn't she? After all, if she lost her balance there was only a three-metre drop, straight into a sewer full of rats. Aaaargh! Mum gathered us all round.

'Listen. When I'm on that beam, it's going to break. It won't break completely, but I'm telling you now so you don't get a shock when it happens. It'll look like I might fall in, but of course I won't. It will make the film look even more exciting. And don't forget: keep absolutely quiet because the crew will be recording.'

Mum took Batpants by the hand and they went to take up their position. I noticed that Cressida Crappletart was no longer hiding round the back. She had come forward so she could see the scene up close. Boy, did she give me the creeps!

7 What Happened Next

Alana glanced around the set. 'Everyone ready? Rescue team on standby?'

Out of the corner of my eye I saw the first-aid crew take up position with a stretcher. I knew this was normal practice, but it didn't exactly make me feel any happier. But then I always get jittery when I see Mum in action. It's scary, but exciting. I reminded myself that Mum had once been in the National Gymnastics Team. Balancing on a beam was like her best subject!

'I'm ready,' Mum called. 'Batpants, time for a ride. Come on.' She offered Batpants her hand. The ape lifted herself on to Mum's back and sat there like some huge, hairy rucksack.

'Go on, Mum!' whispered Finn to himself. 'You can do it!'

'Sssh!' I hissed. My nerves were already jangling like a piano in a multiple pile-up.

Zak tossed back his hair, revealing a deep frown of concentration.

'Cameras one and three on Emma,' ordered Alana. 'Cameras two and four on the beam. Let's roll. Action!'

Mum had a ten-metre run-up. Her eyes were fixed on the plank. She whispered something to Batpants and then began to rock on her feet, backwards, then forwards. 'One, two, THREE!'

Mum sprinted forward. With the weight of Batpants on her back it was hard to accelerate, but Mum had calculated for everything. Meanwhile, I was digging my fingernails into the palms of my hands.

As soon as Mum hit the beam we knew something was wrong. It was wobbling like crazy, but it was impossible for Mum to turn back. She was at full speed.

The beam lurched violently. Mum's foot slipped, she was falling, with the weight of Batpants pulling her down into the rat run. As she fell Mum managed to hook one leg over the beam. She swung loose and locked her other leg over.

Now she was dangling upside down. Batpants lost her grip on Mum's back and was now clinging to her arm with one hand. Below them, hundreds of rats gazed upwards, wondering if lunch was about to arrive. I was sure I could hear the gnashing of sharp little teeth.

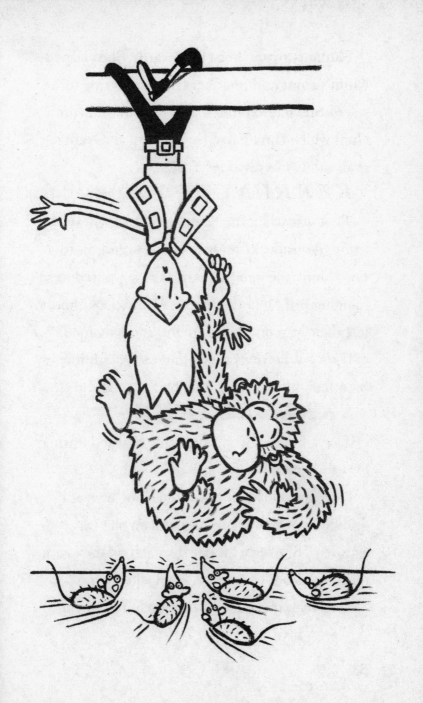

Batpants swung herself upwards. She clasped Mum's chest and then her leg, clambering to safety. She paused to rest her bottom on Mum's chin, which can't have been very nice. Orangutan sandwich, anyone? Yuck.

KERRUNCH!

That was when the beam cracked halfway through, just as Mum had said it would. But I don't think the pair of them were supposed to be hanging from it at that point. Mum's legs almost lost their grip on the beam and she screamed.

For a few seconds they hung there, fighting for breath, fighting to stay attached to the beam.

SKKRRREAKKK!

The splintered wood suddenly cracked further, lowering them deeper into the sewer.

Batpants reached up with her long arm and grabbed the beam. A moment later she was astride it. She lay with her stomach on the beam, reaching down to Mum. They locked hands. Slowly, Batpants pulled Mum up and bit by bit

they made their
way to the far
end of the beam
and safety.

SKKRRRREAKKK!

Mum got to
her feet, held on
to Batpants and
they ran on because
they were still being filmed
until, 'CUT!' cried Alana.
Phew!

The moment filming
stopped, the cheering
broke out and I was able
to breathe again. The
crew were whooping and
throwing hats into the air. Alana was
beaming with delight. Not only had Mum
and Batpants survived, but they had got the best
bit of film ever – even more exciting than what
had been planned.

'Oh boy!' laughed the director. 'You had us worried there, Emma. That was truly nail-biting. Great stuff! Great stuff!'

Zak gave Mum a big hug and whispered in her ear. 'Don't you ever do that again, Mum. I was freaking out.' Then he quickly let her go, tossed back his hair and tried to look the coolest of the cool, with added ice cubes.

And then who should come over to add her congratulations – Cressida Crappletart! That was one big surprise, I can tell you.

'You did well there, Emma. Held your nerve and everything. Glad you're OK.' Cressida nodded quietly and left.

What is she like? Spooky, that's what.

Alana decided they'd had enough excitement for one day and called a halt. The crew cleared away and one by one everybody went, leaving us in the ancient abbey. Silence slowly filled the ruin. I shuddered.

I thought Zak looked really at home in the

gloomy old building, what with his long black coat and purple hair. I could easily picture him drifting about the grounds at night, like a ghastly ghoul, frightening people.

'Let's go,' I said, but Zak held back, gazing at the sewer.

'I'm going to take a look at that beam,' he said. 'I want to know why it wobbled so much.'

'Can't we just go?' I asked. 'This place gives me the creeps.'

'Five minutes,' Zak muttered, and went across to the broken plank. He scraped the ground at the far end with his shoe. Then he bent down and looked more closely. Finally he got to his knees and poked about with his fingers. He pulled at something, got up and walked back to us. He was tossing something up and down in the palm of his hand.

'What is it?' I asked.

'A stone,' said Zak. 'It was under the beam. This is what made it wobble so much. It was enough to put the whole plank out of balance.'

'Great,' I said. 'Can we go now?'

'Sure.'

We left the abbey and headed off. Zak was still tossing the stone around. 'I guess nobody noticed,' he murmured to himself.

Finn and I were busy thinking about what we might be having for lunch. And Batpants was thinking about who knows what? Jam on toast? Jungle stuff?

'I guess nobody noticed,' Zak repeated to himself. 'Unless someone put it there deliberately,' he added quietly.

8 Rhubarb Jelly Fish
La La Belly-buttons

'DELIBERATELY?' I cried. It was impossible
to imagine. Why would anyone do something
like that? 'Zak, you're crazy. Nobody would do
something so dangerous on purpose.'

'I never said they did,' he shrugged. 'Only that
they could have. Either it was an accident or it
was deliberate. I don't know which it was, but,
you know, those special-effect guys spend ages
setting up stunts. I've watched them. They check
everything.'

'OK, so they missed a small stone,' I said. 'It'd
be pretty easy to do that.'

'An animal might have put it there,' Finn
suggested.

I groaned. 'Yeah? Like a badger or a . . .

a crocodile comes along; yeah, a really big crocodile comes along the sewer and thinks, *I'll just push this stone under this log, and when that woman runs across and falls off I'll gobble her up. Yum yum yum.*'

Finn eyed me stonily. 'You're stupid.'

'Well said, Finn,' nodded Zak and turned to me. 'He meant an animal might have kicked it under there without knowing. It's a good suggestion, even if it's unlikely.'

I was beginning to think they were ganging up on me and went into a bit of a sulk. The only thing that cheered me up was knowing that Mum was OK. That was a relief.

On the way home we passed Dad. Mum was there too, watching. Dad was in the big animal pen sharing his lunch with a gorilla. That's the kind of thing he does. Amazing. Dad was sitting there, right opposite this big silverback. Without looking up, he passed a stick of celery across to the ape.

'Why is Dad looking at the ground all the time?' asked Finn.

Mum whispered back. 'You don't look into the gorilla's eyes because they will take that as a challenge, a threat. You look away to show that the gorilla is the boss.'

'So what's Dad doing?' Finn asked.

'He's showing the gorilla that they're friends. He's called Tuesday because he was born on that day. Tuesday's worked with your dad before.

Look, Aslan is grooming him now.'

Dad was slowly going through the fur on Tuesday's back, searching for insects and parasites to be removed. Rather him than me! That gorilla could have torn Dad in half if he wanted. Good thing he didn't want to!

'Is Dad training Tuesday for something?' I asked.

Mum nodded. 'He's preparing him for a scene we're filming tomorrow where Colorado Kate fights a gorilla.'

Zak groaned. 'Mum, you're not going to have to fight a gorilla?'

'I certainly am,' she smiled.

'Why can't Frangelika do it?' demanded Finn. 'Everyone makes a fuss of her, but all she ever does is run about and squeak.'

'*Week-week-week!*' I went in a really high voice. 'I'm Frangelika and I mustn't ever get messy.' I cleaned my nose with a paw-hand, like a mouse.

'She is a bit like that,' laughed Mum. 'But she's

a good actress too. Anyhow, don't worry about Tuesday. There'll be two gorillas. The second one is somebody in a gorilla suit. The crew will film Tuesday first, lumbering towards me, beating his chest and grunting. Then they'll switch to the actor-gorilla and that's who I fight with. It'll be perfectly safe.'

We all breathed a sigh of relief.

'Why can't they do *all* the filming with the gorilla suit?' I asked.

'Good idea,' Mum agreed. 'But it looks more realistic to start with the real gorilla and then change. When we're fighting, everything happens so fast nobody will notice that it's an actor in a suit.'

Tuesday suddenly straightened up and looked directly at us. He didn't look happy either.

'Why is he doing that?' Finn was worried.

'He's spotted Batpants,' said Mum. 'And Batpants has seen Tuesday.'

Batpants grasped the wire fencing and shook it.

She bared all her teeth and grunted as loudly as she could. 'Nugg-nugg-nugg-nugg!!'

'She's angry,' I laughed. 'And look, Tuesday's got to his feet. Why is Dad waving?'

'We'd better take Batpants away,' said Mum. 'She's upsetting the gorilla and your father can't get on with his work. Come on. Let's get back to the caravan.'

By the time we'd walked back Mum was looking shattered. 'I think all that excitement back at the crypt has finally caught up with me. I just need to rest for a bit. I've done nothing about lunch and your father won't be back for a while. Why don't you take yourselves to the mobile canteen? Get something to eat there and ask the guys behind the counter to put it on my account.'

'Fantasti-bubbly-crumbo!' cried Finn. He's always saying that. It drives me potty.

I eyed him stonily. 'Why do you say that? It's rubbish.'

'No it isn't,' protested Finn. 'It's fantasti–'

'*Taisez-vous!*' I yelled, jamming my fingers into my ears.

'Taisez-vous!'

'Think I'll catch up with Lacewing,' muttered Zak. 'I'll get some food later.'

'Lacewing?' echoed Mum.

'His GIRLFRIEND,' I explained with great satisfaction. Smirk smirk.

'No she's not!' snarled Zak. 'Just someone I know, that's all.'

'They're in LURRVE.' I put in, adding lots of kissy noises for good effect.

Zak was about to try to murder me (ha ha, as if!), when Mum interrupted and told us to leave her in peace. Zak sloped off to find his princess while Finn and I wondered what to do. It was too early to go straight to the canteen.

'Let's do something,' suggested Finn. 'We could race my earwigs.'

'Or we couldn't,' I answered.

'OK, we could put all my beetles together and see which is the biggest.'

'Or we couldn't,' I repeated.

'You're not playing at all,' complained Finn.

'I know,' I said. 'I'm bored.'

Fortunately, Batpants rescued both of us. She'd been wandering around for the last five minutes. When she reappeared she was dragging Zak's guitar behind her. She looked

like a failed heavy metal rock freak, but I was the one who freaked out.

'Batpants! Zak will kill you if you even touch his guitar!' I leapt up and took it from her.

'Ploop-ploop,' she complained.

'No, you can't have it back,' I told her, and returned it to Zak's bed. That was when I spotted his hair gel. I went back, waving the jar at Finn. 'Look what I've got. What say we give Batpants a new hairstyle?'

'Fan—'

'Say that word and I'll make you eat this,' I threatened, holding up the gel.

'Crumbo?' squeaked Finn. I had to laugh.

Batpants loved having her hair done. We slapped the gel on her bonce and got to work. It didn't take long for us to tease her hair into great pointy, ginger spikes. Her head was turning into a porcupine. We put more spikes on her shoulders.

'There,' I said, satisfied. I picked up a mirror

so she could see herself.

'Haaaaaaah!' went Batpants, twirling round.
I think she was pleased.

Batpants looked great. It was time to go out
and show her off!

9 Anyone Like a Tomato?

Finn insisted on annoying me by singing
'Fantasti-bubbly-crumbo!' at the top of his voice,
so I drowned him out by shouting 'LA LA LA
LA RHUBARB JELLY FISH LA LA BELLY-
BUTTONS,' and generally spouting nonsense.

Meanwhile, Batpants was lurching along
behind us, walloping the backs of our legs with a

large plant. She must have yanked it out of one of the gardens.

'Hoo hoo whaaaaa!' She sounded like a miniature kung-fu warrior. She looked like one too.

The canteen was a very smart mobile kitchen, full of gleaming stainless steel and spotless pans. Three cooks bustled up and down behind the counter serving a queue of actors, film crew, extras – all sorts. Tables and chairs had been set up on the grass. Cressida Crappletart was there, having a coffee and cramming a large cream

éclair into her mouth.

We picked out some lunch, including a huge salad for Batpants and sat at one of the tables. Batpants was the centre of attention. Everyone was staring at her bizarre hairstyle. Even Frangelika Wotnot looked across and smiled.

'Look!' whispered Finn. 'It's Frangelika! She's having lunch with the director.'

'We could ask for her autograph,' I hinted.

'You ask,' Finn said.

I put on a silly coochy-coochy voice. 'Poor little Finn, are you shy?'

'No. I haven't got any paper,' he answered flatly. 'So nurr.'

I sighed. 'OK, I'll go. I'll take Batpants with me. I think Frangelika reckons she's cute.'

We made our way towards the film star, with Batpants still enjoying a large mouthful of salad. Frangelika took one look at me and turned to the director.

'An autograph hunter,' she declared, 'if ever I

saw one. Am I right or am I right?'

I blushed and nodded. 'If you wouldn't mind. Sorry to disturb your lunch.'

'That's OK, honey,' smiled Frangelika. 'You're Emma's girl, aren't you? I thought so. You know, your mother is extraordinary. She's the best. I wouldn't do her job for all the tea in China.'

'Can you put *To Tilly, Finn and Batpants*?' I asked.

'Sure, honey.'

I guess Frangelika was all right really and, to be honest, I wouldn't have wanted to run through all those cobwebs either. She was really pretty too, with a gorgeous, long white summery dress.

Frangelika turned to Batpants. The orang-utan looked back at her with shining eyes and one finger stuck in the corner of her mouth. Frangelika tried to touch Batpants's hairdo and laughed. 'My, don't you look the business!'

The orang-utan gave the film star an enigmatic smile, took her finger from her mouth, puckered

her lips and then –

RATTA – SPLATTA – TATTA – SPLATTA!

A hail of tomatoes machine-gunned from her mouth, along with the odd bit of watercress and lettuce. Frangelika and Alana were both mown down by the spray of vegetable ammunition.

Frangelika screamed, threw up her arms and toppled backwards. She lay on the ground screaming, with tomato splats all over her dress. Alana remained still and stony-faced. Tomato

juice dribbled from her nose and chin.

Batpants jumped up and down, going 'Hoo hoo hoo hoo!' as if she thought it the funniest thing ever. It pretty much was too! The crew were laughing and I noticed that even Cressida Crappletart was smiling.

I raced round the table to help Frangelika.

'I'm SO sorry. I had no idea Batpants had a mouthful of tomatoes. It's one of her favourite games and Mum keeps trying to stop her and, oh goodness, you're absolutely −' My voice trailed away and finally I said very quietly, '− messed up.'

Frangelika slowly got to her feet. 'Don't touch me,' she snapped. 'Have you seen my dress? It is RUINED! I am going to my caravan for my third shower today and I don't want to speak to anyone.'

To make matters worse Finn hurried across and tried to give her a present by way of saying he was sorry too. He pulled out a matchbox from his pocket. 'Would you like my best beetle?' he

asked, sliding it open and offering Frangelika the
waggling insect.

'AAAARGH!'

Boy, Frangelika could scream in the World
Screaming Championships – and she'd win
hands down. Matchbox and beetle went zooming

through the air as Frangelika knocked it out of Finn's hand. She went steaming off, letting out more screams on the way.

'Don't think she likes beetles,' murmured Finn. 'And that was a really, really good one too. It had pincers this big.'

I glanced at Alana and murmured another apology. She didn't say a word. She simply pushed back her chair, got up and left too. Oh dear.

'See what you've done?' I told Batpants. 'We're in double trouble now.'

One of the nearby film crew called out. 'Hey, she's an orang-utan. She doesn't know it's wrong.'

I looked at Batpants. She gazed back at me for a moment and then flung both arms across her face to hide her eyes.

'Oh yes, she does,' I said. 'Come on, Finn. We'd better get home and start explaining things to Mum before anyone else gets there.'

10 Today is Gorilla Day

Well, we survived the Frangelika and Alana
explosion! In private, Mum thought it was
pretty funny, but she made a big fuss of saying
'sorry' several times and 'it won't happen again',
even though everyone knew it would. I mean,
Batpants *is* an orang-utan, so what can you do?
They don't understand 'sorry' or 'won't do it
again'.

Besides, Mum had more important things on
her mind the next day, like her wrestling match
with a gorilla. Finn and I decided we'd go and
watch, but first of all we were on the trail of our
big brother because guess where Zak was going?
To meet Lacewing, of course! Aah! How sweet.
I don't think. More like yuck yuck yuck. Anyhow,
he was taking his guitar with him, so that meant

he was going to audition her. Zak certainly wouldn't want us there, but there was no way I was going to miss out!

Trouble was, we had a big hairy orange problem.

'Do we have to take Batpants?' I pleaded with Mum. 'We always have to look after her.'

'I don't mind,' said Finn, ever helpful.

'Well I do,' I grumbled.

'Aslan and I are very busy this morning, as you know. Zak's already gone off so I'm afraid that just leaves you two. It's only until the filming is over. I have to go across to the set now. See you later. Be good!'

There was no escape. We were ape-sitters for the morning.

'We'd better camouflage ourselves so we can creep up on Zak without being noticed,' I told Finn. I tied some bushes and foliage around him. We snaffled some of Mum's make-up and splodged over any bits of bare skin we could find. I covered my head with feathers I'd collected and some big leaves.

'What about Batpants?' Finn asked. So I stuck some leaves on top of her head too. Then I got a long piece of string and tied dangly fern leaves all round it so it made a kind of skirt. I strung it round Batpants's waist. She looked like some totally weird hula dancer. Dressing up an orangutan was getting to be fun.

'I heard Zak on his phone,' I told Finn. 'They're meeting up at the empty caravan.'

'Suppose they see us?' asked Finn. 'Won't they be cross?'

I grinned. 'Probably, but it'll be worth it. Anyway, I want to hear Lacewing sing, don't you?'

Finn shrugged. He's got no sense of romance, that's the trouble. We set off, slipping through the trees and darting from one bush to another. We hardly saw a soul and it didn't take us long to reach the caravan.

Finn and I tiptoed up the steps to the door and crouched outside. We could hear them talking, but not loud enough to tell what they were saying, so that wasn't going to be any good. The caravan was standing on concrete piles that put the windows well above our level of eyesight.

I spotted an old wheelbarrow not far from the caravan. 'That's perfect! We can put it under a window and stand on that,' I suggested.

As I wheeled it over I was just in time to see
Batpants disappearing on to the roof of the
caravan. How on earth had she got up there?
Still, there was nothing I could do about it and
besides, I really wanted to see what Zak and
Lacewing were up to.

I parked the barrow beneath one of the
windows. It wobbled a
bit as we climbed in,
but we managed
OK and soon we
were edging our
noses over the
bottom of the
window.

Zak was standing
on the
other side
of the
caravan
with some

97

music propped up on the window ledge, playing his guitar. Lacewing was at the other end of the room, singing. Actually, she was quite good. Maybe even more than good. They were going through one or two songs they both knew from their favourite bands.

'That's not bad,' said Zak. 'How do you feel?'

'Bit nervous,' admitted Lacewing. 'I've never auditioned for a band before.'

'I think we should try some of the Non-Organic Vegetable numbers now,' Zak suggested. 'I've only got this sheet with the words and music so you'd better stand beside me.'

I grinned at Finn. 'I bet he kisses her!'

'Urgh,' he muttered, pulling a face and screwing his eyes shut. 'That's revolting. I'm not going to watch.' That's what Finn said, but I saw he kept one eye open!

Lacewing had moved across to Zak's side. She leant over him to read the music.

'Did you write this song?'

'I'd rather not say,' Zak answered, and she laughed.

'That sure means you did! You're clever.'

They looked at each other for a couple of seconds. It was only two or three seconds, but it was THAT LOOK. You know, the dopey one, the TOTALLY SOPPY ONE. Zak started playing and Lacewing sang.

> '*I saw you the first time, your hair was black and long,*
> *And when I got home I sat and wrote this song.*
> *Can't get you out of my mind, can't get you out of my brain,*
> *If you won't go out with me I think I'll go insane.*'

That's moody Zak for you, always exaggerating. Anyhow, Lacewing was impressed. After she'd finished singing they looked at each other again. It wasn't a couple of seconds this time. It was like a whole minute of silent gazing into each other's eyes and then . . . and then they moved closer, and CLOSER and CLOSER.

SSSSTTTTTPPPPPPPPPP!!!!

That's meant to be the sound of a long kiss, just in case you hadn't worked it out.

Which was immediately followed by:

KERRBLAMM-A-SPLANNGGG!

Which was the sound of Batpants falling off the roof of the caravan, clutching wildly at the guttering and then smashing against the window next to us. Finally, she lost her grip and fell into the wheelbarrow.

The wheelbarrow was completely unbalanced. Finn went tumbling to the ground with a loud shout of 'HELP!' while I clung with my fingertips to the window ledge, looking straight at Lacewing and Zak. Lacewing screamed, probably thinking some war-painted leafy monster from the woods was out to get her, not

to mention the upside-down orang-utan in a fern hula skirt.

Then I had to let go. BLUMMPP! It was my turn to fall to the ground. The door of the caravan crashed open and Zak came thundering out.

'I might have known it was you two!' he shouted.

'It was Batpants!' I yelled back.

'I'll tell Mum you were spying, you little toerag,' Zak threatened.

'So? I'll tell Mum you were snog-snogger-snoggering. Didn't you have breakfast this morning?'

'I think some of my ants got squashed when I fell off the wheelbarrow,' Finn announced sadly, pulling a flattened matchbox out of his pocket.

Meanwhile, Batpants was running around, pulling fern leaves from her skirt and throwing them at us.

'Look at the three of you,' Zak went on. 'What do you think you look like?'

Lacewing pulled at Zak's arm. 'Come on. Forget about them. They're just kids. It's time to go and see your mom and the gorilla.'

Somehow she managed to calm Zak down. He scowled at us several times and they set off. We trailed after them at a safe distance and only caught up when we reached the film set.

Dad was there to help with Tuesday the gorilla. Alana wanted to film Tuesday rushing at Colorado Kate. After that, the plan was to replace the real gorilla with an actor in a gorilla suit and then the wrestling match would take place. It was supposed to end with the gorilla dragging Colorado Kate away.

Oh horror! What would happen next! Would Kate be torn to shreds by the gorilla or would she survive to film yet another adventure about Colorado Kate?

(ANSWER: Of course she would otherwise there would be no more Colorado Kate adventures, would there? Do those film-makers think we're dumb, or what?)

The film crew didn't often have a real gorilla a few metres away so they were quite excited. The set itself was the ruined abbey again, with its creepy, ivy-covered walls. Tuesday had her own special cage round the back of the abbey. Colorado Kate was meant to be searching the abbey for a clue to the mystery when the gorilla would attack her.

Every safety precaution had been taken. The whole set was surrounded by a high wire fence so if the gorilla didn't obey Aslan's commands he would be contained by the pen. A marksman with a stun-dart rifle was on standby and would shoot Tuesday if necessary, but it would take five minutes or so for the sedative to work.

'It won't come to that,' Dad had promised. 'Tuesday will do exactly as she's asked. All Emma has to do is the fight with the actor in the suit. Cressida is doing that. They've worked together before.'

Cressida Crappletart! It would have to be her of all people, wouldn't it? Huh.

There was one last bit of filming to do before the crew were ready. Dad was inside the pen. He was using a clicker and a large bucket of fruit to get Tuesday lumbering towards him. Animal handlers use a clicker to train the animal. When it does what you want it to do, you click the clicker and give the animal a reward, like some fruit. The animal soon learns what to do.

So Tuesday was plodding towards Dad. Then he suddenly held out both arms wide and clicked the clicker. This was the signal for Tuesday to stop. They filmed the same bit three times before the director was happy.

'Thanks, Aslan. Tuesday can go back to his cage now. We'll have Emma and Cressida next for the fight scene. Ready in ten minutes, please.'

'Come on,' said Finn. 'We've got time to whizz round the back.'

'What for?' I asked.

'To see Tuesday, of course, close up. He might like to see my collection of earwigs.'

'I doubt it,' I said heavily. 'He can probably give you a few bugs of his own, though.' I sighed. 'OK, I'll come with you, but only if someone can look after Batpants. Last time Tuesday saw her she got a bit uppity.'

'We'll take her for a walk,' offered Lacewing, and Batpants happily took the hand she offered, giving it a thorough lick.

Lacewing winced. 'Actually, Batpants, I did have a shower this morning, you know.'

'You did offer to take her,' warned Zak. 'Let's walk her over there.'

Finn and I hurried towards the back of the abbey. It was a long way round because we had to skirt behind the pen. By the time we got there Dad had shut Tuesday in his cage and gone back to join the crew. The gorilla was standing in his cage looking a bit puzzled, but at least he had a banana to take his mind off things.

'He's amazing,' murmured Finn. 'I've never been so close to one. Not even in a zoo.'

'We live with one,' I pointed out, thinking of Zak. 'Come on, we can't stand here forever gawping at a gorilla. Mum's going to be doing her bit any second and I want to see it. Let's get back.'

I turned to go, but Finn wasn't behind me. When I looked back he was standing frozen, staring at the cage. Inside I could see there were now two gorillas. TWO?

And then one of them pulled off its head.

11 Go, Batpants, Go!

It was Cressida Crappletart! What was she up
to? She was supposed to be wrestling with Mum.
I shoved a hand over Finn's mouth and dragged
him down to the ground.

'MMMMM-MM-MMMMM?!' That was
what he tried to say.

'Shush. I'm sure Cressida Crappletart's up to
something. Keep quiet and we'll creep nearer.'

It's not much fun crawling through the
undergrowth, I can tell you. You've got stones
and sharp twigs sticking in your knees, plus I had
little brother punching my bottom.

'I can't see ANYTHING because your bum is
MASSIVE.'

'It is NOT massive.'

'It is. It's bigger than Jupiter and that's the
biggest planet in the –'

'Will you pipe down!' I hissed back. 'I want to
see what's going on.'

'Planet-bum,' muttered Finn, and then he went
quiet at last.

Cressida carefully slid back the bolt on the
gorilla's cage. She let the door swing open and
then hurried out of harm's way. Tuesday stepped
from the cage. Now he was in the abbey grounds

where Colorado Kate was supposed to be hunting for clues to the Mystery of the Crimson Chameleon.

The great ape stood there, wondering what to do with himself. That was when Cressida picked up a stone and flung it at the gorilla's head. Ouch! That was nasty. Tuesday gave a roar of pain and blundered forward wildly, disappearing into the abbey, while Cressida vanished back among the trees.

'Mum' I gasped. 'We've got to warn Mum!'

We took off round the edge of the abbey. We had to run right round the outside of the pen, racing and panting, tripping over our feet. As we neared the film crew I saw that it was already too late.

Tuesday was in a rage and heading for Mum. Dad was in the pen too, frantically clicking and waving his arms, but Tuesday was too angry to take any notice. The gorilla saw Mum crouching on the ground, searching for clues, and made straight for her. Mum of course thought it was Cressida.

'Emma!' yelled Dad. 'Get out! It's Tuesday!'

'Somebody stop him,' I cried.

The marksman was already in position. There was a muffled bang and the dart hit Tuesday. But he was still raging forward and it would all be too late.

Suddenly, there was a noise of crashing cameras and overturned chairs. I wheeled round to see what it was. Batpants! Boy, was she angry! She was showing all her teeth and chattering with rage.

'Nugg-nugg-nugg-nugg-nugg!!'

She came hurtling through the crew, sending everything in her path tumbling to the ground. People leapt out of her way. Cameras toppled over. Chairs went flying. So did one or two people as they dived for cover.

Batpants went charging into the pen, her arms going round like windmills, hollering like some crazy beast. 'HOO HOO HOOOOEY HOOOOOOO!' I'd never seen her run so fast. (Actually, I'd never seen her run!)

She headed straight for Tuesday, hooting and howling like a steam engine thundering out of a tunnel. And then, just as Tuesday was about to grab Mum, Batpants leapt into the air and hurled herself at the great ape. She landed with her full weight, her feet punching into the gorilla's chest.

For a few moments Tuesday was winded and

very surprised. In those vital seconds Batpants
climbed up the ape's back, sitting astride his
shoulders with her hands firmly over his eyes.
Tuesday began to shake his head and pull at

Batpants, who was a lot smaller than the gorilla.
But Batpants clung on, shrieking, while Tuesday
roared and raged and shook his furious head.

Dad sprinted across and helped Mum to safety.

By the time they were back outside the pen, Tuesday's movements were getting weaker and more sluggish as the drug took effect. Finally, he slumped to the ground in a deep sleep.

Batpants climbed on to the gorilla's chest and held up her hands in triumph. The film crew rose to their feet, cheering and clapping, whooping and whistling.

And then the questions began. How had the gorilla escaped? Surely Dad had shut him away?

Cressida Crappletart appeared, rubbing her head. 'What happened?' she asked. 'I took up my position and the next thing I knew I was lying on the ground by Tuesday's cage, the door was open and he'd gone. What's been going on?'

'The gorilla must have knocked you out cold,' someone suggested. 'He's dangerous.'

'Doesn't sound like Tuesday,' murmured Dad. 'He's a gentle giant normally.'

'It wasn't Tuesday,' Finn shouted, pointing straight at Cressida. 'It was her!'

The stuntwoman laughed loudly. 'You've got to be kidding. Don't be crazy. What are you saying about me?'

'Finn's right.' I said. Boy, I was so angry I could hardly speak. You know how people sometimes say they're boiling with rage? Well, I felt like I'd explode with heat!

'We went round the back to see Tuesday. We'd almost left when Cressida arrived in her costume. She took off her head. She let Tuesday out and then threw a stone at him. That's when he went charging out. We both saw it.'

'You can't believe them!' yelled Cressida. 'They're kids! What do they know? They're just jealous because I'm a better stuntwoman than – than – HER!' she spat at last, glaring at Mum.

Mum looked at Cressida in disbelief. 'Why would you want to do that, Cressida? I might have been killed.'

'Because I should have your job. I'm better than you and everyone knows it! I should be Colorado Kate's stuntwoman, not you!'

Everyone looked at Cressida in shocked silence. Batpants offered her own little burp of shock. 'Uuuurp.'

Alana called across several security guards. 'Take Cressida to her caravan and keep her there until the police come.'

118

'Uuuurp.'

Cressida was escorted away, still yelling that she
should have been Colorado Kate.

We could talk about nothing else for the rest
of the day. Alana called an end to filming for the
time being. Everyone was too stunned. The crew
drifted away, talking quietly to each other. Dad
was busy with Tuesday, making sure the gorilla
came round safely from the tranquillizer. Mum
was checking that Batpants was OK.

Zak had his arm round Lacewing and was holding her close. He saw me looking and scowled.

'I'm comforting her,' he growled. 'She's upset.'

I gave Zak my most serious and caring look. 'You'd better kiss her better then, hadn't you?' And just to help I added the right sound effect.

SSSSHHHTTPPPPPP!

11 and a bit
The Disgusting End

Mum was pretty shaken by the whole business. In fact, everyone was edgy.

'Maybe it was Cressida who made the beam over the sewer wobble,' Zak suggested.

'What?' Dad swung round.

'Can't prove it,' Zak went on. He put a hand in his pocket and pulled out the stone. 'Tilly and Finn and I took a look at the beam when nobody was around. This stone was underneath one end. It unbalanced the whole thing – you know, like a table with one leg shorter than the others. I dunno, maybe the special effects guys did it.'

Mum shook her head. 'The crew would never have done anything as crazy as that. The plank was carefully designed to almost break, not to

wobble. You've no idea how much care those guys take over things like that. Our lives are at risk when we do stunts. Everything has to be thought through.'

She shook her head again. 'No, someone put that stone there. We can probably never prove it was Cressida, but I think you're right, Zak. Clearly she's mad enough to do something like that.'

'So it wasn't a hungry crocodile then?' asked
Finn, throwing me a scowl.

Dad hugged Mum closely. 'The main thing
is you're OK. We're all OK,' he added, smiling
back at us.

At that point, Batpants wandered in wearing
a tea towel on her head and carrying a large
saucepan.

'Heeee-heeeeeee,' she said.

'She's hungry,' I interpreted.

'She's always hungry,' laughed Mum, handing the ape a banana.

Zak cleared his throat and announced that he was off to find Lacewing.

'Lacewing?' repeated Dad as the door shut behind Zak. 'Isn't that an insect?'

'Girlfriend,' Finn and Mum chorused.

'Latest,' I added. 'You know what he's like. He sees a girl and he's in love. Again. Still, if they get married we could all move to Hollywood.'

Mum and Dad were puzzled. 'How do you work that out?' asked Dad.

'Lacewing is Frangelika Wotnot's daughter. Zak's going out with a film star's daughter! How peachy is that! Yay!' I punched the air.

Mum placed a gentle hand on my shoulder. 'Tilly, I'm sorry to disappoint you, but, firstly, have you forgotten Zak is thirteen? He's not marrying anyone for quite some time yet.'

I shrugged. 'I can wait.'

'Maybe, but there's something else you should know,' Mum went on. 'Lacewing is not Frangelika's daughter. She is the daughter of Alana.'

'Honestly, Zak's useless,' I muttered. 'Can't he get anything right? He was supposed to be going out with Frangelika Wotnot's daughter, not the director's.'

'But you were the one who said she was Frangelika's daughter,' Finn pointed out. 'Zak never said.'

I glared at my little brother. 'Finn, why don't you go and do something useful, like count your earwigs?'

'OK,' said Finn, and off he went happily. Honestly, sarcasm is wasted on the young. So that's two useless brothers I've got. That left me with Batpants. She was the only sensible one around.

I looked at her. 'Thank goodness you're clever,' I told her.

Batpants threw one arm round my shoulders. Then she shoved what was left of her banana into my left ear.

SPLURRRPPPPPP!

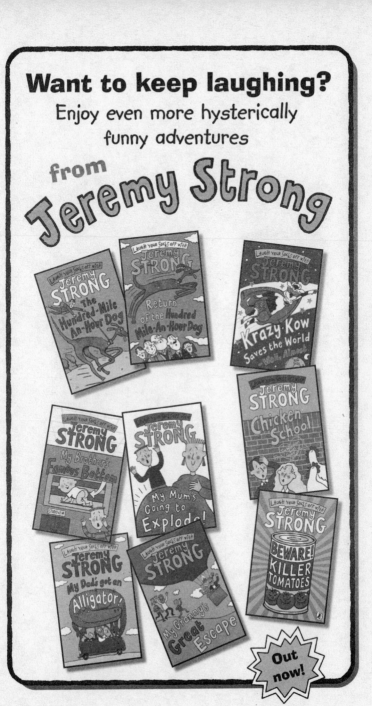

14½ Things You Didn't Know About

Jeremy Strong

* * * * * * * * * * * * * * * * * * * *

1. He loves eating liquorice.

2. He used to like diving. He once dived from the high board and his trunks came off!

3. He used to play electric violin in a rock band called **THE INEDIBLE CHEESE SANDWICH**.

4. He got a 100-metre swimming certificate when he couldn't even swim.

5. When he was five, he sat on a heater and burnt his bottom.

6. Jeremy used to look after a dog that kept eating his underpants. (No – **NOT** while he was wearing them!)

7. When he was five, he left a basin tap running with the plug in and flooded the bathroom.

8. He can make his ears waggle.

9. He has visited over a thousand schools.

10. He once scored minus ten in an exam! That's ten less than nothing!

11. His hair has gone grey, but his mind hasn't.

12. He'd like to have a pet tiger.

13. He'd like to learn the piano.

14. He has dreadful handwriting.

And a half . . . His favourite hobby is sleeping. He's very good at it.

Log on and laugh for hours!

Brand-new 100-mile-an-hour amusement at the KRAZY KLUB.

CRAVING MORE SILLINESS? Join Jeremy's **KRAZY KLUB** at jeremystrong.co.uk

With hilarious new features:
- Prove how KRAZY you are!
- Addictive games!
- Streaker's blog!

Plus:
Fab Competitions • Fun Stuff • Sneaky Previews
Interactive Polls • Hot Gossip

 and lots more rib-tickling treats!